PAULA REGO
Nursery Rhymes

PAULA REGO

Nursery Rhymes

Introduction by
MARINA WARNER

Thames and Hudson
1994

First published in Great Britain in 1994
by Thames and Hudson Ltd, London
First published in the United States in 1994
by Thames and Hudson Inc.,
500 Fifth Avenue, New York, New York 10110
by arrangement with The Folio Society

British Library Cataloguing-in-Publication Data

A catalogue record for this book is available from the British Library

Library of Congress Catalog Card Number 94.60933

ISBN 0–500–01649–6

Typeset in Scotch Roman at The Folio Society
Printed in Great Britain by The Bath Press Colourbooks
on Banbury Wove paper and bound in quarter cloth
with printed sides at The Bath Press, Avon

Contents

Mother Goose and Paula Rego

Marvels mix with the day-to-day and banality meets mystery in the nursery rhyme: an English genre of nonsense verse almost unknown in the rest of Europe, nursery rhymes are now preserved as written literature. But once upon a time they were a common kind of speech, like prayers or jokes, charms or curses. The meanings of most have been forgotten, though the inspired sleuthing undertaken by folklorists like Iona and Peter Opie has solved some of the enigmas. When we speculate who Mary Mary quite contrary might be (Mary Queen of Scots?) or which King was in the counting house counting out his money (Henry VIII?), we realise that the spell of the rhyme lies elsewhere. The classic nursery rhyme's simplicity is funny ('The cow jumped over the moon') and can raise goosebumps (those 'three blind mice'); the very ordinariness of the verse attaches it to daily, general experience, brings it into everyone's back garden, as it were, where it flips over into the oracular. To be uncanny – *unheimlich* – there has to be an idea of home – *heimlich* – in the first place – but a home that's become odd, prickly with desire, and echoing with someone's laughter.

Paula Rego has had many homes and they return in her art, which she makes in the same way as she used to play in her room in Portugal as a child: on the floor, with toys and dolls around her to help her imagine. Her paintings have been inspired by the stories told her by her grandmother and her aunt and a maid in the country near Lisbon where she grew up, her stern heroines – little girls with bows in their hair intent on their household tasks – recall the female paragons in the moral tales of the Comtesse de Ségur (*Les Malheurs de Sophie*), which Paula Rego was read when she was their age. With her paintings, she enters that disturbing gap between the portrayal of the heroine's perfections and the wicked feelings stirring inside oneself. Paula Rego's little girls owe something to the Surrealists' cult of the *femme-*

enfant, to Max Ernst's heroine in his collage novel, *Histoire d'une petite fille qui voulut entrer au Carmel*, and to Balthus's spectacle of young girls' intimacies. But Paula Rego does not come as an outsider to the scene; nor as a seducer. She has said of her work that 'suddenly it's as if a dog were to tell its own story', for she is speaking from inside, she is telling tales she knows, from a place – a home base – generally over-looked, the female child's. She not only hears the 'dog', she becomes it. Nursery rhymes are populated with fabulous, talking creatures, with wooing frogs and laughing dogs, for children and animals have always liked one another, and even been confused by their elders, subjected alike to maltreatment on the one hand, petting and spoiling on the other. The universe of children is subject to adults' authority, and brimful of the potency ascribed to instinct, to irrationality, to pre-social (antisocial?) behaviour. Paula's husband, the artist Victor Willing, identified her characteristic themes as 'domination and rebellion, suffocation and escape', recognisable conditions of childhood, and especially of girlhood in the Fifties in Salazar's Portugal. Paula Rego has always identified with the least, not the mighty, taken the child's eye view, and counted herself among the commonplace and the disregarded, by the side of the beast, not the beauty. But she has also confronted, even celebrated, the powers emanating from this quarter: hers are not simplistic tales of victims and oppressors at all, but constantly surprise the viewer with unexpected reversals. Her sympathy with *naïveté*, her love of its double character, its weakness and its force, led her to nursery rhymes as a new source for her imagery.

At the age of ten Paula Rego was sent to an English school, where she recited the verses for the first time. Now, with a four-year-old granddaughter, she has rediscovered them for a series of etchings which she executes as a child might, spontaneously, drawing directly on to the plate without preparatory planning of any kind. On purpose, she hasn't distanced herself from illustration, because she wanted to retrieve what is usually considered a humble artistic category and pay tribute to Victorian artists like John Tenniel, who created Alice, the goblin painter Arthur Rackham, and Beatrix Potter, who also loved animals and took their part – against gardeners. Like them, she treats

8

the fantastic realistically, dresses animals in human costume, and introduces dream-like dislocations of scale. The rhymes attracted her too because she's a specialist in using humour as a means of confronting terror: 'I paint to give fear a face', she has said. Like Goya, whose ghost haunts this sequence of prints, she can be viciously comic: her nursery rhymes are also capriccios, about folly and delusion, cruelty, convention, and sex, communicated with disturbing glee.

Mother Goose's Melody, the first printed collection, appeared in about 1768: the name Mother Goose was borrowed from the French, specifically from Charles Perrault's collection of fairytales of 1697, *Contes du temps passé, ou Contes de ma mère l'oye*. Mother Goose is an imaginary figure, an old crone who passes her wisdom on to children, often bypassing grown-ups altogether. She's the voice of Granny, of Nan, of nursemaids and governesses, remembered from childhood. She can be comical – like a goose – and slightly sinister, like a white witch; she's a mother, who feeds her flock with stories and nonsense; she's female because speech is the realm of those who cannot read and write, like children, and like peasants and women in the past. Iona and Peter Opie, collecting skipping rhymes and other nonsense verse in playgrounds up and down England for their great work on children's play *The Singing Game*, found that it is only little girls, between the ages of four and fourteen, who transmit skipping and hopscotch rhymes and invent new ones. Paula Rego has taken up that tradition, and turned it into potent visual images.

The uniforms of post-war Portugal return, costuming her soldier mannikins and imperturbable aproned Misses like national dolls. The particular circumstances of her upbringing, under the twin regimes of the Catholic Church and military dictatorship, provide a structure of sexual oppositions which emerge again very powerfully in the riddling pairs in the nursery rhymes: Miss Muffet and the spider, Polly and her officers' tea-party, Baa Baa Black Sheep and the questioner, even Old King Cole and his fiddlers three. By remembering the separation of men and women's spheres in her birthplace, and the different obligations of manhood and womanhood, Paula Rego has reinterpreted familiar, innocent verses with a post-Freudian mordancy. The very

9

meaninglessness of the rhymes gives them fluid and multiple meanings, for which the artist has conjured a certain unmistakeable atmosphere: they have become a theatre where the child anticipates ambiguous dramas of sexual curiosity and conflict. In these prints (engravings) Paula Rego has seized hold of Mother Goose, the magnificent body of oral literature, and transformed her through private memory and imagination.

Marina Warner

PAULA REGO
Nursery Rhymes

Humpty Dumpty

Humpty Dumpty sat on a wall,
Humpty Dumpty had a great fall.
    All the king's horses,
    And all the king's men,
Couldn't put Humpty together again.

Jack and Jill

Jack and Jill went up the hill
  To fetch a pail of water;
Jack fell down and broke his crown,
  And Jill came tumbling after.

Up Jack got, and home did trot,
  As fast as he could caper,
He went to bed, to mend his head
  With vinegar and brown paper.

Baa, baa, black sheep

Baa, baa, black sheep,
   Have you any wool?
Yes, sir, yes, sir,
   Three bags full;
One for the master,
   And one for the dame,
And one for the little boy
   Who lives down the lane.

See-saw, Margery Daw

See-saw, Margery Daw,
Johnny shall have a new master;
He shall have but a penny a day,
Because he can't work any faster.

Little Miss Muffet

Little Miss Muffet
Sat on a tuffet,
Eating her curds and whey;
There came a big spider,
Who sat down beside her
And frightened Miss Muffet away.

Ride a cock-horse

Ride a cock-horse to Banbury Cross,
To see a fine lady upon a white horse;
With rings on her fingers and bells on her toes,
She shall have music wherever she goes.

Mary, Mary, quite contrary

Mary, Mary, quite contrary,
  How does your garden grow?
With silver bells and cockle shells,
  And pretty maids all in a row.

Who killed Cock Robin?

Who killed Cock Robin?
I, said the Sparrow,
With my bow and arrow,
I killed Cock Robin.

*All the birds of the air
Fell a-sighing and a-sobbing,
When they heard of the death
Of poor Cock Robin.*

Who saw him die?
I, said the Fly,
With my little eye,
I saw him die.

Who caught his blood?
I, said the Fish,
With my little dish,
I caught his blood.

Who'll make the shroud?
I, said the Beetle,
With my thread and needle,
I'll make the shroud.

Who'll dig his grave?
I, said the Owl,
With my pick and shovel
I'll dig his grave.

Who'll be the parson?
I, said the Rook,
With my little book,
I'll be the parson.

Who'll be the clerk?
I, said the Lark,
If it's not in the dark,
I'll be the clerk.

Who'll carry the link?
I, said the Linnet,
I'll fetch it in a minute,
I'll carry the link.

Who'll be chief mourner?
I, said the Dove,
I mourn for my love,
I'll be chief mourner.

Who'll carry the coffin?
I, said the Kite,
If it's not through the night,
I'll carry the coffin.

Who'll bear the pall?
We, said the Wren,
Both the cock and hen,
We'll bear the pall.

Who'll sing a psalm?
I, said the Thrush,
As she sat on a bush,
I'll sing a psalm.

Who'll toll the bell?
I, said the Bull,
Because I can pull,
I'll toll the bell.

Old Mother Hubbard

Old Mother Hubbard
Went to the cupboard,
To fetch her poor dog a bone;
But when she came there
The cupboard was bare
And so the poor dog had none.

She went to the baker's
To buy him some bread;
But when she came back
The poor dog was dead.

She went to the undertaker's
To buy him a coffin;
But when she came back
The poor dog was laughing.

She took a clean dish
To get him some tripe;
But when she came back
He was smoking a pipe.

She went to the alehouse
To get him some beer;
But when she came back
The dog sat in a chair.

She went to the tavern
For white wine and red;
But when she came back
The dog stood on his head.

She went to the fruiterer's
To buy him some fruit;
But when she came back
He was playing the flute.

She went to the tailor's
    To buy him a coat;
But when she came back
    He was riding a goat.

She went to the hatter's
    To buy him a hat;
But when she came back
    He was feeding the cat.

She went to the barber's
    To buy him a wig;
But when she came back
    He was dancing a jig.

She went to the cobbler's
    To buy him some shoes;
But when she came back
    He was reading the news.

She went to the seamstress
    To buy him some linen;
But when she came back
    The dog was a-spinning.

She went to the hosier's
    To buy him some hose;
But when she came back
    He was dressed in his clothes.

The dame made a curtsy,
    The dog made a bow;
The dame said, Your servant,
    The dog said, Bow-wow.

Hey diddle diddle

Hey diddle diddle,
The cat and the fiddle,
The cow jumped over the moon;
The little dog laughed
To see such fun,
And the dish ran away with the spoon.

Rub–a–dub–dub

Rub–a–dub–dub,
Three men in a tub,
And who do you think they be?
The butcher, the baker,
The candlestick–maker
Turn 'em out, knaves all three.

Three blind mice

Three blind mice, see how they run!
They all ran after the farmer's wife,
Who cut off their tails with a carving knife,
Did you ever see such a thing in your life,
    As three blind mice?

Mother Goose

Old Mother Goose,
    When she wanted to wander,
Would ride through the air
    On a very fine gander.

Goosey, goosey gander

Goosey, goosey gander,
    Whither shall I wander?
Upstairs and downstairs
    And in my lady's chamber.
There I met an old man
    Who would not say his prayers,
So I took him by the left leg
    And threw him down the stairs.

Ladybird, ladybird

Ladybird, ladybird,
    Fly away home,
Your house is on fire
    And your children all gone;

All except one
    And that's little Ann
And she has crept under
    The warming pan.

Rock-a-bye, baby

Rock-a-bye, baby, on the tree top,
When the wind blows the cradle will rock;
When the bough breaks the cradle will fall,
Down will come baby, cradle, and all.

Polly, put the kettle on

Polly, put the kettle on,
Polly, put the kettle on,
Polly, put the kettle on,
    We'll all have tea.

Sukey, take it off again,
Sukey, take it off again,
Sukey, take it off again,
    They've all gone away.

Old King Cole

Old King Cole was a merry old soul,
And a merry old soul was he;
    He called for his pipe,
    And he called for his bowl,
And he called for his fiddlers three.

Every fiddler had a fine fiddle,
And a very fine fiddle had he;
    Oh, there's none so rare
    As can compare
With King Cole and his fiddlers three.

How many miles to Babylon?

How many miles to Babylon?
Three score miles and ten.
Can I get there by candle-light?
Yes, and back again.
If your heels are nimble and light,
You may get there by candle-light.

Hickety, pickety

Hickety, pickety, my black hen,
She lays eggs for gentlemen;
Gentlemen come every day
To see what my black hen doth lay.
Sometimes nine and sometimes ten,
Hickety, pickety, my black hen.

Sing a song of sixpence

Sing a song of sixpence,
    A pocket full of rye;
Four and twenty blackbirds,
    Baked in a pie.

When the pie was opened,
    The birds began to sing;
Was not that a dainty dish,
    To set before the king?

The king was in his counting-house,
    Counting out his money;
The queen was in the parlour,
    Eating bread and honey.

The maid was in the garden,
    Hanging out the clothes,
When down came a blackbird,
    And pecked off her nose.

A frog he would a-wooing go

A frog he would a-wooing go,
  Heigh ho! says Rowley,
A frog he would a-wooing go,
Whether his mother would let him or no.
  With a rowley, powley, gammon and spinach,
  Heigh ho! says Anthony Rowley.

So off he set with his opera hat,
  Heigh ho! says Rowley,
So off he set with his opera hat,
And on the road he met with a rat,
  With a rowley, powley, &c.

Pray, Mister Rat, will you go with me?
  Heigh ho! says Rowley,
Pray, Mister Rat, will you go with me,
Kind Mrs Mousey for to see?
  With a rowley, powley, &c.

They came to the door of Mousey's hall,
  Heigh ho! says Rowley,
They gave a loud knock, and they gave a loud call.
  With a rowley, powley, &c.

Pray, Mrs Mouse, are you within?
  Heigh ho! says Rowley,
Oh yes, kind sirs, I'm sitting to spin.
  With a rowley, powley, &c.

Pray, Mrs Mouse, will you give us some beer?
  Heigh ho! says Rowley,
For Froggy and I are fond of good cheer.
  With a rowley, powley, &c.

Pray, Mr Frog, will you give us a song?
    Heigh ho! says Rowley,
Let it be something that's not very long.
    With a rowley, powley, &c.

Indeed, Mrs Mouse, replied Mr Frog,
    Heigh ho! says Rowley,
A cold has made me as hoarse as a dog.
    With a rowley, powley, &c.

Since you have a cold, Mr Frog, Mousey said,
    Heigh ho! says Rowley,
I'll sing you a song that I have just made.
    With a rowley, powley, &c.

But while they were all a-merry-making,
    Heigh ho! says Rowley,
A cat and her kittens came tumbling in.
    With a rowley, powley, &c.

The cat she seized the rat by the crown,
    Heigh ho! says Rowley,
The kittens they pulled the little mouse down.
    With a rowley, powley, &c.

This put Mr Frog in a terrible fright,
    Heigh ho! says Rowley,
He took up his hat and he wished them good-night.
    With a rowley, powley, &c.

But as Froggy was crossing over a brook,
    Heigh ho! says Rowley,
A lily-white duck came and gobbled him up.
    With a rowley, powley, &c.

So there was an end of one, two, three,
    Heigh ho! says Rowley,
The rat, the mouse, and the little frog-ee.
    With a rowley, powley, &c.

The old woman who lived in a shoe

There was an old woman who lived in a shoe,
She had so many children she didn't know what to do;
She gave them some broth without any bread,
And whipped them all soundly and put them to bed.

Ring-a-ring o' roses

Ring-a-ring o' roses,
A pocket full of posies,
  A-tishoo! A-tishoo!
We all fall down.

There was a man of double deed

There was a man of double deed
Sowed his garden full of seed.
When the seed began to grow,
'Twas like a garden full of snow;
When the snow began to melt,
'Twas like a ship without a belt;
When the ship began to sail,
'Twas like a bird without a tail;
When the bird began to fly,
'Twas like an eagle in the sky;
When the sky began to roar,
'Twas like a lion at the door;
When the door began to crack,
'Twas like a stick across my back;
When my back began to smart,
'Twas like a penknife in my heart;
When my heart began to bleed,
'Twas death and death and death indeed.

The grand old Duke of York

Oh, the grand old Duke of York,
    He had ten thousand men;
He marched them up to the top of the hill,
    And he marched them down again.

And when they were up, they were up,
    And when they were down, they were down,
And when they were only half-way up,
    They were neither up nor down.